RIVER PARADE

ALEXANDRA DAY

RIVER

PARADE

PUFFIN BOOKS

ACKNOWLEDGMENTS
My special thanks to Tom and Nathan Adams
for their patient cooperation, and to
Rabindranath Darling and Theodore Andrews
for their toy-making help.   —A.D.

PUFFIN BOOKS
Published by the Penguin Group
Viking Penguin, a division of Penguin Books USA Inc.,
375 Hudson Street, New York, New York 10014, U.S.A.
Penguin Books Ltd, 27 Wrights Lane, London W8 5TZ, England
Penguin Books Australia Ltd, Ringwood, Victoria, Australia
Penguin Books Canada Ltd, 10 Alcorn Avenue, Toronto, Ontario, Canada M4V 3B2
Penguin Books (N.Z.) Ltd, 182–190 Wairau Road, Auckland 10, New Zealand

Penguin Books Ltd, Registered Offices: Harmondsworth, Middlesex, England

First published in the United States of America by Viking Penguin,
a division of Penguin Books USA Inc., 1990
Published in Puffin Books, 1992
3   5   7   9   10   8   6   4   2
Copyright © Alexandra Day, 1990
All rights reserved

LIBRARY OF CONGRESS CATALOGING-IN-PUBLICATION DATA
Day, Alexandra.
River parade / by Alexandra Day.   p.   cm.
"First published in the United States of America
by Viking Penguin . . . 1990"—T.p. verso.
Summary: When a young boy goes for a boat ride on the river and
accidentally falls in, he finds that swimming is not as frightening
as he expected.
ISBN 0-14-054158-6
[1. Swimming—Fiction.   2. Boats and boating—Fiction.]
I. Title.
PZ7.D32915Ri   1992   [E]—dc20   91-33434

Printed in the United States of America
Set in Baker Signet

One afternoon it was so hot that all I felt like doing was watching the fan. Then my father said, "Let's go for a boat ride on the river." I said, "Okay, as long as I don't fall in."

I got Laurel, Upstairs, and Buoyant.

We drove to the river.

Dad helped me put on a jacket that would float.

The river was bigger than I thought it would be.

The boat was nice.
I liked the smell and the sound of the river.

All of a sudden, Laurel fell in.
I yelled out, but he liked it.

Dad put a string on him.

I looked down at the fish.
They looked up at me.

I knocked Buoyant into the water,
and he liked it, too.

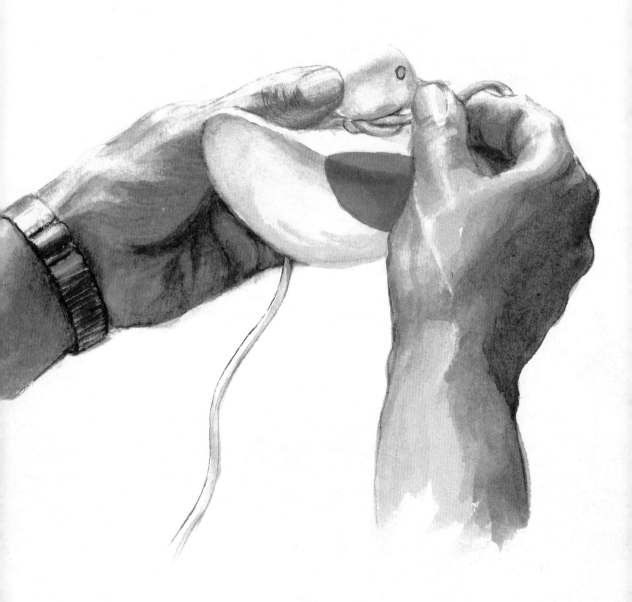

Dad tied him to the string.
Now I had two.

The river got narrow and noisy.

All of a sudden Upstairs jumped in.

We grabbed him just in time
and added him to the string
when the water got calm.

I reached over to move a branch
and then I was in, too.

It was cold and nice.
We were like a parade.
It's wonderful to swim
in the river,

as long as you're on a string.